JOSH likes art class and phys. ed., prefers his grubby jeans to his Sunday best . . . and gets around in a wheelchair.

AIMEE rides a scooter, baby-sits her younger brothers, has a dog named Scrappy . . . and is blind.

JAMIE has curly brown hair, loves to play charades . . . and can only ''hear'' you by reading your lips.

These three kids may have some handicaps, but they don't want your sympathy—they just want to be friends. Once you get to know them, you may be surprised at how much you have in common!

MEET MY

Friends

JONI EARECKSON TADA

Chariot Books™
David C. Cook Publishing Co.

Chariot Books™ is an imprint of David C. Cook
Publishing Co.
David C. Cook Publishing Co., Elgin, Illinois 60120
David C. Cook Publishing Co., Weston, Ontario
Nova Distribution Ltd., Newton Abbot, England

MEET MY FRIENDS
© 1987 by Joni Eareckson Tada for text and Julie Durrell for the interior
illustrations. All rights reserved. Except for brief excerpts for review purposes, no
part of this book may be reproduced or used in any form without written permissio
from the publisher.

Cover illustration by Mel Williges
Cover design by Elizabeth Thompson

First Printing, 1987
First Printing, New Edition, 1993
Printed in the United States of America
98 97 96 95 94 93 5 4 3 2 1

Library of Congress Cataloging-in-Publication Data

Tada, Joni Eareckson.
  Meet my friends.
  "Chariot books."
  Summary: In this collection of three stories, young Christians find the strength to
overcome their phisical handicaps.
  1. Children's stories, American. [1. Physically handicapped—Fiction. 2. Christiar
Life—Fiction. 3. Short stories] I. Durrell, Julie, ill. II. Title.
PZ7.T116Me 1987   [Fic]   8722344
ISBN 1-55513-808-X

When I was your age, I didn't know anyone in a wheelchair. I didn't know anyone who was blind. And the only person I knew who had a hearing problem was my Uncle Dick—and even that I hardly noticed, unless he forgot to wear his hearing aid.

The only time I ever saw a disabled person was when Mom and I would go shopping downtown on a bus. On the corner of Howard Street, a blind man always sat on a stool with a cup of pencils in his hand. His coat was tattered, and he had a collie beside him who looked like he wanted to be petted. I felt sorry for the blind man. In fact, I felt bad for all the disabled people I had never even met!

But then everything changed. Suddenly, I was the one in a wheelchair, as a result of breaking my neck after diving into shallow water. At first I was scared and lonely. I was afraid that people would feel sorry for me, just as I had felt sorry for the blind man on Howard Street.

But God changed everything. When I

put my life in His hands, I no longer felt scared and lonely. Jesus became my very best Friend, and He introduced me to a lot of other friends—some disabled like me and others on their feet like you. I was glad to learn that being in a wheelchair was nothing to be sorry about. It was the start of a new and exciting adventure.

While on this adventure, I've met so many special friends. I'd like to introduce you to a few of them. The kids you will meet in this book are not made up. The events which happened to them are not pretend. Three of them—Kristen, Camille, and Aimee—are grown-ups now, and we work and play together a lot. Their real-life stories are the inspiration for the children you will get to know here.

You'll find that Aimee, Josh, and Jamie are a lot like you. They have fights with their little brothers, want to be liked by their classmates, wear faded Levis, and love God.

So let's begin right now, because I want you to Meet My Friends!

THE IRON MAN

The alarm blasted and I fumbled for the off button. As soon as peace and quiet settled over my bedroom, I moaned and sank back into my pillow. It was the beginning of the second yucky week at my new school, Hillcrest Elementary. *I wish I were back at my old school,* I fumed, throwing back my covers, *with my old friends in my old fifth-grade class!*

Before I had my pajama top unbuttoned, Mom was in the room, gathering my shirt and pants from the closet.

"Mom, please . . . not those icky pants I wear to church. I want to wear my jeans. The real faded ones.''

''Joshie, not again! You've worn those jeans three days in a row.'' Mom rummaged through the pile of shirts, sweats, and underwear I'd stuffed in the corner. ''And how many times have I told you to put your dirty things in the hamper?''

Moms—they're always telling kids to pick up this and put away that. And they're always making up cutesy weird names like ''Joshie.'' I wish she'd just call me Josh like all my old friends.

''Do you want to wear your new Reeboks?'' she interrupted my thoughts.

''Nah. Tommy hasn't had a chance to get them nice and dirty yet.'' My brother, Tommy, is not your average stick-in-the-mud little brother. Actually, he is a neat little guy, especially when it comes to helping me break in a new stiff pair of jeans or scuff up a pair of tennis shoes so the soles will look walked on. Oh, yeah, I should explain—I'm in a wheelchair. Surprised? Well, don't let it hang you up.

I've been in a wheelchair since I was a little kid, and it's really not that bad. That is, as long as I've got friends who understand. Which brings me back to Hillcrest Elementary School.

Tommy and I chowed down breakfast and headed out the door. Tommy could have taken the bus, but he decided to ride with me in Mom's car. Like I said, Tommy's not bad for a third grader.

While Tommy finished his spelling homework, I doodled on my book covers. Mom, as usual, talked the whole way to school. Was my teacher assigning kids to help me? Did I have enough help during lunch? Was my classroom accessible? I don't know why she worries so much; I'm not a little kid anymore. And I can handle life—even fifth grade—in a wheelchair.

"—and are you making new friends, Joshie?"

I knew it would make her worry more, but I decided to be straight with her.

"Mom, you don't know what it's like at Hillcrest. I've been there a week, and I still don't know anybody. I hate being the new kid!'' Right away, I wished I hadn't told her. Now she would baby me.

But Mom did something that really surprised me. She didn't say anything. Finally, Mom spoke, but in a different tone.

"Joshua, we can't help it that Daddy's work brought us to a new neighborhood. Remember our prayers last night?''

I nodded. It had felt good to pray.

"We asked God for new friends at Hillcrest. And we asked Him to help you to be brave.''

Mom was right. I did pray those things. But as we pulled up to the front of Hillcrest Elementary, I didn't feel too courageous. Tommy helped unfold my wheelchair, waved, and ran off to his class. There it sat, my new zippy sports chair—black and chrome—gleaming in the sun. It had a low-slung, leather back, new super ball bearings on the racing wheels, and black, foam grips on the handles. With orange flame decals on the sides, it looked more like a supermodified formula racer. I didn't care what anybody thought—I was proud of my wheels!

Mom grabbed the waistband of my jeans and hiked me out of the car and into the wheelchair. She did some nice ''mother things'' like roll up the cuffs of my jeans and loosely lace my shoestrings the way the other kids did.

''Mom, I'm sorry. I don't mean to make you worry. It's just that, well. . . . There's a girl in my class who wears braces, and they call her Tinsel-Teeth Tammy.'' I grabbed hold of the metal rim of my wheels. ''Who knows what jerky name they'll come up with for me?''

Mom did what she always does when we have these honest talks about my disability. She knelt by my wheels and stroked my hair like she did when I was a baby. ''Mo-o-om!'' I put on a whine, glad that Tommy wasn't around to see. But it did feel good.

I jostled around on my seat cushion to get comfortable, piled my books on my lap, slung my duffel bag over the handle of my chair, and started off. With a hard shove, my chair and I coasted down the ramp to the school entrance. Putting on my bravest smile for the kids hanging around the flagpole, I recognized one of the boys from my class. Johnson—I didn't know if it was his last name or a nickname. But there was no chance to ask. The kids broke up and walked away as I came near. I was hoping Johnson would hold the front door open for me, but he disappeared by the time I got there. It was a good thing Mom had decided to visit the school office; she caught up with me and held open the door. I wheeled into the noisy, crowded foyer.

"Bye," I called and turned my wheelchair toward the hallway. The smile on Mom's face was one that meant: "Josh, you know I would like to help." She always felt that way. But our family was used to letting me face my own problems, even though I was still a kid.

My wheels made squeaky sounds on

the shiny linoleum and a couple of boys
carrying backpacks turned around to look
at me. I flashed them a smile, but they
only moved aside to give me passing
room. Then I noticed that half the kids in
the hallway had parted like the Red Sea. I
felt six feet wide.

"Watch out for your toes, guys," I
teased as I glided past the boys with
backpacks. I hoped they'd chuckle back,
but nobody said anything to me. There

was just the usual before-school chatter about skateboards and Atari games and what was on the Disney Sunday movie the night before.

I got to class early and pushed aside a couple of empty desks to get to my place. I stacked my books—Dad had helped Tommy and me cover our books with brown, paper grocery bags over the weekend. That's what the kids did at Hillcrest, and we wanted to fit in. I reached into my duffel bag and pulled out my homework on diagramming sentences. As I was going over my work, I noticed Johnson waltz in, cracking gum and shuffling baseball cards. He wadded his gum and tossed a sky hook toward the wastebasket. Instead it hit Tammy's desk.

"Sorry, Tinsel-Teeth. Must be those magnets in your mouth," Johnson said flippantly as he picked his gum off her desk. I felt really bad for her.

For a second, I thought he looked my way. I smiled, but he quickly flopped into his seat with his back to me. I sighed, grabbed my pencils, and began wheeling toward the line at the sharpener in the back of the room.

"Oh, let me get out of your way," a girl in a sweat shirt and high-topped tennis shoes said, stepping aside.

"Hey, no problem. You're fine where you are," I answered. But I think she was afraid to look at me. She just kept talking real fast to her friend who was wearing the same kind of sweat shirt and tennis shoes. *Girls,* I thought. *All they care about is stupid photographs of TV stars and Barbie dolls—and each other.* The morning was off to a winner of a start. I decided I wouldn't say anything else in line.

Most of the day was yucky—just like the week before. I did everything everyone else did: I wheeled my chair up front to write on the blackboard, I was able to fit down the aisles to help pass out papers, I could reach for the plants by the windowsill to help water them. I even tried to share my chocolate chip cookies, but only one kid took them, and he acted like the cookies had cooties. I pulled out my G. I. Joes and matchbox cars from my duffel bag during recess, but all the other guys wanted to play dodge ball. I tried to crack a few jokes, but no one really thought they were funny. Except for one person. . . .

It was during lunch. A boy named Harold (and that's what everybody called him, not Hal or Harry, but Harold) was asked by our teacher to carry my lunch tray from the cafeteria line to the table. I hadn't noticed him much in class, except that the rest of the kids enjoyed picking on him. I guess that's because Harold got lots of A's, especially in science. He was interested in dinosaurs and carried a picture of a Tyrannosaurus Rex in his wallet. He drew pictures of the solar system on his book covers and always laced his tennis shoes up tight instead of leaving them undone.

But I liked him. I don't know, maybe I felt sorry for him, too. I guess getting picked on is a lot worse than being ignored. Besides, Harold seemed genuinely glad to carry my tray, even though he was assigned the job.

Could Harold be God's answer to prayer for a good friend at Hillcrest? Naah! At least, I hoped not. I wasn't sure I wanted to hang around Harold too much—I might get picked on, too. But it *was* nice to have someone to talk to. And as I said, he liked my jokes.

"Hey, Harold," I said as I slapped the seat next to me, inviting him to sit and eat his lunch. "You know what they say about my wheelchair?"

Harold bit into his sandwich and shook his head no.

"I'm into heavy metal."

Harold laughed so hard he spit bologna and lettuce all over the table. I thought I might like him after all.

"So what's with the other guys?" I reached in my lunch bag for what was left of my chocolate chip cookies. "Nobody seems to want to make friends around here.'' I looked at the empty seats near us and then at the crowded tables around the rest of the cafeteria.

''It's not so bad,'' Harold said with his sandwich in his mouth again. ''At least we're always guaranteed a place to sit at lunch.''

I threw my last cookie back in my bag along with the rest of my trash. ''Forget it. Kids in this school act like they've never seen a wheelchair before.''

Harold took a long time, chewing and thinking. ''You, at least, they ignore. Me, they pick on.'' He paused again. ''I think most kids just feel they need to pick on somebody.''

I thought of Tinsel-Teeth Tammy and looked at Harold as he wiped his mouth with the back of his hand. ''Who made up that rule?'' I muttered as I unlocked the brakes to my chair.

We finished lunch and lined up with the rest of the class to head for art. Of all the things about Hillcrest school, I liked art and phys. ed. the best. Mrs. DePesto

18

made art so much fun. Today we were going to design posters for next week's Junior Olympics.

"Hey, need a push?" I heard a girl say behind Harold and me. I looked over my shoulder and saw a blonde-haired girl with a single long braid. I knew that her friends—the girls in sweat shirts and tennis shoes—called her Kerrie. But she wasn't like the other dumb girls; she acted more like a guy. I liked her.

In art class, Mrs. DePesto divided us up into groups of three to work on Junior Olympics posters. I didn't say it, but I was glad that Kerrie was assigned to work with Harold and me. In no time we had paste, colored paper, poster paints, and glitter everywhere.

"How about this for a poster title—'Make Tracks for the Junior Olympics!'?" I suggested.

"Uh . . . sure," Kerrie said. "But I don't get it."

"Me, neither," chipped in Harold.

"You'll see," I said with a sly grin.

"Harold, hand me a brush. Kerrie, lift that paint can up here, will you?" They shrugged their shoulders at each other and followed through. I dipped my brush deep into the paint and began slapping the color on my wheels.

They looked at me as though I had bananas for brains.

Then, "He-e-ey," said Harold, as though a light bulb had gone on over his head. "I get the idea!" He and Kerrie grabbed brushes and began to carefully cover every inch of tread on my wheels.

Kerrie spread sheets of poster board in front of and behind my chair. "Okay, I'll get in the front. Harold, you grab the back." Kerrie pulled while Harold pushed. I leaned over to catch a look. Bright red tracks silk-screened a bunch of tire tread patterns on yellow poster board. They pushed and pulled my wheelchair over five other sheets of board, each a different color.

"All right!" Harold exclaimed, wiping his hands on his pants.

20

"Not bad," Kerrie said, as she let out a low whistle.

The rest of the class had put down their scissors and paste to see what we were up to. Thankfully, Mrs. DePesto thought our posters were tops. I could tell that most of the other kids were impressed, too. All except Johnson and his buddies—it was plain they weren't interested in posters of Junior Olympics.

When the 3:30 bell rang, Tommy and I were out on the curb, waiting for Mom. I didn't see Kerrie or Harold anywhere. I had wanted to tell them thanks for being such good sports in art class, and for, well . . . being *almost* friends.

That night, Tommy jabbered on and on at the dinner table about the snake his friend brought in for show and tell. I decided to keep my art class triumph to myself for the time being. Fifth grade was beginning to look a little brighter at Hillcrest Elementary, but there was still a long way to go.

On the way to school the next day,

Mom hardly had a chance to get a word in edgewise. Tommy and I traded stories about our teachers, the cafeteria food, recess, and the Junior Olympics. I could tell Mom was relieved *not* to hear whining.

At lunchtime, Harold was there again to help me carry my tray. We had a lot to talk about—where the posters should be hung and which Junior Olympic events we should try out for.

After lunch we lined up as usual. Today was my other favorite class—phys. ed. Coach Brubaker would be testing our entire class for next week's Olympics. We'd be competing with kids from Milford Elementary School in events like the hundred-yard dash, the softball throw, and the long jump.

"Hey, Harold," yelled one of the boys from the back of the line, "maybe Coach Brubaker has an event just for you—the dinosaur dash!"

Here we go again! I groaned to myself.

"Stegasaurus, Brontosaurus,

Tyrannosaurus Rex—Harold smells as gross as a dinosaur's breath.''

"Back off, Johnson," I heard a girl say behind us. I looked over my shoulder and saw Kerrie holding a softball and glove. For a second I thought I saw her smile at Harold and me, but maybe she was only cracking gum. I turned around and began wheeling my chair, following the rest of the kids to phys. ed. I liked Kerrie. She stood up for Harold even when I couldn't—or, should I say, didn't.

Outside on the playground, Coach Brubaker separated us into groups. A few kids went to the track to be tested, and others, including Kerrie, headed for the softball diamond. I parked my wheelchair under the basketball net, leaned over to pick up a ball, and began turning it over in my hands while waiting for Coach to decide what to do with me.

"Harold, you'll stay in this group." Coach Brubaker pointed with his whistle toward me and a few others who were hanging around under the net. Looking at the others, I realized our group was made up of kids who weren't very good at sports. I was always getting stuck with kids who weren't athletic, but that didn't bother me. Coach Brubaker had no way of knowing how strong I was or how well I could dribble or shoot a basket—or even how fast I could wheel my chair.

I gave Harold a big grin. We were becoming a regular duo. I bounced the ball to him.

Coach Brubaker made each of us stand behind the foul line and shoot baskets. He was really surprised when I made eight out of my ten tries. Harold, on the other hand, couldn't make even one. He stuffed his hands in his pockets and kicked at the blacktop.

Just then Johnson and some of his buddies walked by the basketball court on their way in from the track. "Hey, Harold, why don't you try standing on a ladder . . . even you can make baskets that way!" They held their sides, doubling over in laughter.

I didn't see what was so funny. Feeling my face get red, I knew I had to get away from there before I exploded. Without thinking, I gave my wheels a hard shove and raced toward a basketball. As my chair whizzed by it, I stretched to reach for the ball. "Oh, no . . ." I felt my wheelchair tip. I was falling.

Crash!!

"Help! Coach Brubaker!" I could hear Harold yelling.

Nobody was laughing anymore. Instead, I could feel their eyes on me. I knew I wasn't hurt, or at least I didn't think I was. Falls like these have happened a lot.

"Joshua, are you all right?" Coach Brubaker said as he helped me sit up. "Harold, go get Josh's chair."

"Aaaaw." I rubbed my elbow and glanced at the kids standing around. A few turned their backs. Some pretended nothing happened. Johnson just stared. It dawned on me that they were more embarrassed than I was. I not only felt embarrassed, I felt sick. And suddenly, I felt angry. Not at the kids so much. I was angry at my paralyzed legs. And I was angry at God.

"Here, let me," Harold said as he locked the brakes on my wheelchair and grabbed my legs. He and Coach Brubaker helped me back into my seat. Their smiles made me feel a lot better.

"Those . . . those bean brains," Harold grumbled, casting an angry glance at Johnson, who was dribbling a basketball with his buddies at the other end of the court. "Who needs them?"

I knew exactly what Harold was feeling. I had felt like that zillions of times, for as long as I could remember. But being angry at other kids just because they tease you or, in my case, ignore you, just doesn't cut it. Also, I had learned that feeling down on myself or God got me nowhere. I sighed deeply. I had to come up with a whole new plan of action.

"Harold, we are not going to give up," I said, as I wiped the dirt off my hands.

26

"Huh?" Harold looked blank.

"Coach Brubaker," I said. "I've got an idea!"

The next day our teacher gave her okay. For the next few days Coach Brubaker came to get Harold and me out of class early.

"Hey, where are you guys going?" Kerrie whispered, as I wheeled past her desk toward the door. I smiled at her. I wished I could let her in on our secret, but Harold and Coach and I had agreed. It would be a surprise.

"How come they get out early?" Johnson sneered.

"Yeah, what's going on?" a couple of others demanded.

No way was I going to give a clue. I plopped my books on my lap and buzzed out the door with my best smug look. After Coach clicked shut the classroom door behind us, Harold and I let out a whoop and headed for the gymnasium.

• • •

The day of the Junior Olympics finally

arrived. Bright and early, several buses from Milford Elementary pulled up to the front of Hillcrest. Kids piled out of the buses with their softball bats and gloves, track shoes, school banners, and lunch bags. As our school bell rang, kids from every class poured out the doors and organized into teams on the field. Johnson and his buddies headed for the track. I gave the thumbs-up sign to Kerrie, who headed for the softball diamond with her ball and glove. I whipped my chair around; kids were cheering everywhere. For the first time in weeks I began to feel a little bit of Hillcrest school spirit.

Coach Brubaker handed Harold and me stopwatches and clipboards. "You boys know what to do, right? Make certain that the boys and girls who are competing are properly listed. Write down their numbers. Get their accurate times. Okay?" He checked off a list on his clipboard. "You boys will make good statisticians."

"Stati-what?" I said, squinting.

"Just ask Harold," Coach smiled.

Harold was deep in paperwork. He kept pushing his glasses back on his nose with one hand and scribbling names and events while balancing a clipboard on his lap with the other. Numbers and figures. He was right at home with his job.

I draped a whistle around my neck and pulled down a visor over my eyes. "Ready?" I called to Harold as I stuffed the event sheets in my duffel bag and wheeled toward the playground.

"Ready!" he said as he gathered his papers and followed, giving the leather back of my wheelchair a slap.

We wheeled over to the long jump area, watched the competition, and collected the results. Milford won that event. The sun was getting high in the sky as we headed for the softball diamond to check out the game. Hillcrest was ahead by two runs. The tension was high as the two schools split for lunch.

Next were the track events. Milford ran away with the high jump. Hillcrest topped the hurdles. The results so far were split down the middle. We watched Kerrie win the softball throw. Harold and I quickly compared our numbers—her win put Hillcrest ahead by one event. But Johnson didn't win the hundred-yard dash as he hoped—and Milford and Hillcrest were now tied.

"Way to go," Harold muttered at Johnson who was bending over, still wheezing.

"Well, let's see you get on the track and do better, Mr. Stupid-Scorekeeper," Johnson spat back.

"Oh, yeah?"

"Hey, lighten up." I jabbed Harold good-naturedly in the side.

"Well, he's always—"

"Doesn't matter." I lowered my voice. "We're in this together, okay?"

Harold adjusted his glasses as he adjusted his attitude. I didn't mean to scold him. It's just that I had tried that old trick of giving others a taste of their own medicine. It always backfired. But now, something *was* about to work, and work big! It was time for our secret plan!

"Okay, you two." Coach Brubaker herded us toward the chin-up bar on the playground. "Josh, your event is the next and last."

"Josh has an event?" Kerrie asked, surprised.

"But he's a . . . a handicap," one of Johnson's friends protested.

I handed over my whistle and visor to Kerrie. She didn't say anything, just smiled and gave me her thumbs-up sign.

Milford and Hillcrest kids parted to let us through. This time it felt kind of good to imagine myself six feet wide.

"Coming through. Stand back, everyone." Harold played the role of a playground monitor.

I gave my sports chair a big shove and coasted past the assembled classes.

"Come on, Hillcrest, three cheers for Josh!" I heard Kerrie yell behind me. A couple of kids whooped and hollered. But neither she nor the rest of my classmates

really knew what was up. I hoped I would
be able to pull it off!

I stopped short of the chin-up bar.
Milford's top kid was already on his fifth
chin-up. I kneaded the muscles in my
hands as I watched the muscular boy
strain toward ten chin-ups.

Milford began to get rowdy. "Come
on! Hang in there! Go for it!"

The Milford boy began to shake as he
sweated and jerked toward twelve.

"Keep going! Keep going!" A couple of kids waved banners and flags.

Thirteen.

Fourteen.

The boy let out a groan as his chin crested the bar for the fifteenth time. He dropped to the sand, exhausted. Immediately he was surrounded by his cheering friends. He had tied the Junior Olympic record for the fifth grade.

"Good going," I said as I stretched my hand toward him with a broad smile.

He wiped his hands on a towel and confidently stretched his hand toward me. I couldn't help but be amazed at the natural way he returned my handshake. Here he was a stranger, and yet he accepted me right off. My own classmates didn't even do that.

The moment was over too quickly. It was my turn.

"Give him room; give him room." Coach spread his hands as Harold helped me position my chair directly underneath the chin-up bar.

"Ready?" Harold rubbed his hands together.

I took a deep breath, squinted shut my eyes, and prayed silently. *Please, God, help me not to be a show-off. You've given me strong arms to push a chair. Now let these arms show the kids the gift You've given me. And, er, it would be nice to win. Uh, that is, I mean . . . win new friends.*

I opened my eyes. There was my little brother Tommy. He had squeezed his way through the crowd to the edge of the sand. I gave him a wink. He tried his way of winking back—blinking both eyes.

I rubbed my sweaty palms on my jeans. Harold and Coach Brubaker hoisted me out of my chair and held me still until I could grab the bar tightly. "Ready!" I said, and they let go. Immediately I felt the weight of my paralyzed legs pull me down. The muscles in my arms stretched.

With a mighty heave, I flexed. My body rose and I completed my first chin-up. I heard a smattering of applause from the Hillcrest kids. Although my legs hung limp, my upper body twisted as I kept chinning quickly up to number eight. From then on, it was going to be a real contest.

"Number nine!" a couple of Hillcrest kids began to chant.

I felt the years of pushing my wheelchair begin to pay off. "Number ten!" the chant spread throughout the Hillcrest crowd.

"Number eleven!" Tammy didn't seem to care about spitting through her braces every time she cheered. "Number twelve!" I relaxed for a moment, letting my body weight stretch my arms. My hands burned. My shoulders ached. Sweating and straining, I continued. "Number thirteen!" I heard Tommy screech. *Thanks, God!* I said to myself as I felt the cold metal of the bar underneath my chin again.

"Come on, Josh!" Kerrie jumped up and down. Suddenly I felt a surge of energy. My pace quickened. "Number fourteen—fifteen—Josh has got the Junior Olympic record tied!'' Hillcrest kids were wild with excitement.

"He's going for an all-class record." Coach Brubaker looked at his clipboard. "Sixteen—seventeen!"

My smile expanded and I almost giggled. I was about to surprise everyone, including myself. "Eighteen—nineteen!" By this time even Milford was cheering me on. The kids were jumping up and down in a frenzy.

"Twenty chin-ups . . . a state record!" Coach Brubaker threw his visor in the air, and a tremendous cheer went up from the entire playground. Kerrie was doing cartwheels. Harold and Tammy were actually hugging each other.

My fists felt frozen to the bar. "Hey, you guys, somebody get me down," I managed between gasps. Immediately Harold and Coach wrapped their arms around my knees and lowered me to my chair as though it were a king's throne. It felt so good to sit down!

As I blew on my hot hands, somebody handed me a towel. I smashed my sweaty face into it; then I looked up. Johnson.

"You're pretty tough," he said with a cocky smile. "You're a real iron man."

"Hey, yeah, Iron Man," Harold said, slapping me a high five.

A nickname . . . an honest to goodness nickname—besides Joshie.

"Hey, Iron Man," someone shouted from the middle of the crowd, "where'd you learn to chin-up like that?"

"My coach—Coach Hal. Right, Hal?" I grinned and winked at Harold, who stood there a little dumbfounded. Coach Brubaker crooked his arm around Hal's neck and tousled his hair.

"Not bad, Hal," Johnson said. "You're not as nerdy as I thought."

Hal blushed.

The crowd began to thin as kids headed for the awards ceremony in front of the bleachers by the softball diamond. We had won the Junior Olympic trophy.

I let my little brother push me to the

softball field. Harold carried my duffel bag, and Kerrie strolled beside me.

"Next thing you know, the guys will be lining up a mile deep to arm wrestle you," she said.

I chuckled. "Iron Man. Hmmm . . . Feels nice to be accepted."

"You think it was just because of your chin-ups?" Kerrie asked.

I gave her the sort of knowing smile I had often seen my mom give me. I knew the inside story. Everybody—Tammy, Coach Brubaker, even Johnson—felt better about seeing not only me in a new light, but Harold, too. It had become cool *not* to pick on somebody. Or to ignore.

I gathered Tommy in my arms and hoisted him up on my lap. With a hard shove, we went careening down the path to the softball field. The cool, late afternoon air rushed through my hair. I leaned my head back and breathed a sigh of relief. *Thanks God—You did it. Answered prayers and more friends than I can count!*

FRIENDS ON CANWOOD STREET

My name is Aimee and I live on Canwood Street, the most beautiful street in town. It's especially nice this time of year—the oak trees are full of leaves, and the weather is warm enough to ride my scooter. Mrs. Gardner, four doors up, has roses growing over her picket fence, and Mr. Espey, next door, always gives our family a bag of his home-grown tomatoes. Canwood Street is a perfect place to live—except for Grandpa Dudley across the street.

Grandpa Dudley isn't really my grandpa, but Mom told me to call him that out of politeness. He's nice enough, I suppose, but there are times when I don't feel like being very polite to him. Like this morning . . .

"Hi, there, Aimee!" Grandpa Dudley called as he raked leaves in his front yard. I stopped my scooter at his curb. "You sure do ride that thing well for a handicapped girl."

"Yeah," I mumbled as I swiveled my handlebars.

That's what I didn't like about Grandpa Dudley. He always called me "handicapped." Handicapped people use wheelchairs or are retarded. And I am *not* in a wheelchair, nor am I retarded. I felt like telling that to Grandpa Dudley.

I heard the scratch of his rake, and I knew he had gone back to his yard work. I listened carefully for cars and then gave my scooter a shove. I coasted across the street to our house, where I knew Mom was in the backyard hanging laundry.

"Mom," I said, as I leaned my scooter up against our fence, "do you think I'm handicapped?"

40

I could tell she was shaking out damp towels; they smelled so wet and fresh.

"Well, yes and no, Aimee. You are handicapped when people don't let you do things you know you *can* do." She stopped, probably to think for a minute. "You're handicapped when your teachers forget to . . . let's say, type your papers in Braille. But for the most part, honey, I don't think of you as handicapped. And neither do Daddy or your little brothers."

Mom drew me close against her apron

and gave me a big squeeze.

I rubbed my eyes as she held me in her arms. I know you're going to think this is strange, but my eyes aren't like yours—they're made of glass. But you would never know; in fact, they never look tired or red and are a pretty color of blue, my mother tells me.

Mom went back to her laundry, and I sat on the back porch steps with Scrappy, my scruffy-looking gray-haired dog. I love Scrappy—he licks my cheek whenever I feel sad. And I was never sadder than when I lost my eyesight because of something called *retinal blastoma*. Scrappy came to live with us then. I may have lost my sight, but I was glad I got him. Maybe one day he'll be my guide dog.

I held Scrappy for a long time, thinking about what Mom had said. "I don't care what Grandpa Dudley thinks," I whispered into Scrappy's ear. "I am *not* handicapped. Oh, I crash into my fair share of trees and poles when I'm not paying attention, but I can roller-skate and ride my scooter like most kids."

I turned Scrappy's face toward me. Stroking his forehead, I continued, "Somebody just has to show me the street a few times, and I'm on my own. I can even feel if there's a parked car in the way." I stopped for a minute. "*Except* if it's a windy day, or if I have a cold. Then I don't have very good balance. Scrappy, what do you think? Does that makes me handicapped?"

He licked my cheek, just as I knew he would.

The next day I gathered my papers for my science report and left early for school. I've walked to school a hundred times before, and I know every crack in the sidewalk. Maybe I was handicapped when I was first learning the way, tripping and stumbling. But after running into the fire hydrant at the corner of Canwood and Oak a few times, I'm a lot more careful. I even know where Mrs. Gardner's thorny rosebush sticks out over the fence. *I-AM-NOT . . . HAN-DI-CAPPED,* I repeated to myself, keeping a rhythm as I walked.

The school halls were really crowded, and I had to concentrate hard to use my "radar" so I wouldn't bump into anyone. I better explain that—my "radar" (or facial vision, as my doctor calls it) helps me feel when something is near me. That's how I can find my seat in the classroom, walk around a telephone pole on the way home, or even swerve to avoid Mrs. Gardner's bushes. Last year in the third grade I tried using a cane, but I decided I didn't need it. People say I have unusually good radar. Maybe that's because I lost my sight when I was a little kid instead of a baby.

I made it to my classroom with minutes to spare.

"Hi, Aimee," Judy called from her seat. Judy is my best friend. By the echo in her voice, I could tell our classroom was still mostly empty. I waved hello in her direction.

"Are you ready to give your report today, Aimee?" Mrs. Collins asked as she was writing on the chalkboard.

"I sure am, Mrs. Collins," I said as I placed my duffel bag by my desk and felt for my chair. I like my teacher a lot. She and the teacher's aide type a lot of my assignments in Braille—little bumps in patterns on plain white pages. I run my fingers over the bumps and can feel each word. My books are big and bulky compared to the nice, small books my classmates use. When I walk down the hall, I always carry my books in a duffel bag so no one will see how big they are.

Mrs. Collins likes me so much it's a little embarrassing. I don't want her treating me special in front of the other kids. I have to admit it is nice, though, when she lets me pass out papers, water the plants, or help put up bulletin boards. Sometimes when she loses things on the floor—little things like paper clips or pins—I help her find them. My fingers are totally sensitive. But speaking of sensitive things, there's one person in my class who is anything but. . . .

"Hey, Aimee, who dressed you this morning? You have on one pink sock and one brown!" That was weirdo Alan.

"Alan, that will be enough," Mrs. Collins said sternly.

Dumb Alan. He was always trying to trick me into thinking my blouse was polka-dotted and my skirt was striped. As usual, I knew he was wrong. I had checked my socks before I put them on this morning—I could tell by feeling if I had the right ones. But just to double-check, I reached down to feel once more, pretending to scratch my ankle.

Later that morning, during our science unit, it was time to give my report on clouds. I gathered my duffel bag and notes and slowly made my way to the front of the class. I was so nervous that I wasn't paying attention and ran into Jared's desk. I heard snickering from the direction of Alan's seat. But I felt better once I was holding on to the podium. Mrs.

Collins helped me spread out my notes.

Running my fingers nervously over the pages, I looked straight ahead and delivered my speech about the differences between cumulus, cirrus, and stratus clouds. I read a quote about cloud seeding from my Braille science book— underlined with staples so I could find it easily. Then I pulled out a wad of cotton balls from my duffel bag.

"I think clouds must look so soft and fluffy, that if we could touch them, they might feel like this." I passed handfuls of cotton balls down each row. "Close your eyes and imagine what you have in your hands is part of a real thunderhead," I instructed the class.

The room was quiet while each student slowly handled the cotton.

"Wow . . . Yeah . . ." a couple of kids said. I breathed a big sigh of relief. My report was over.

As I sat down and the next student began to give his report, I heard someone behind me say, "Pssst."

A note was shoved into my hand. I ran my fingers over the underside of the paper and felt the impression of the hard-penciled words.

Your report was <u>neat</u>!
Love,
Judy

Judy and most of the kids in class were my very good pals. All except weirdo Alan. I was getting tired of his stupid jokes. Yesterday when I brought my Braille spell writer into class to take notes, he had something smart to say.

"Yikes . . . what's *that* thing?"

"It's a bomb!" I snapped back at him. "If you don't watch it, I'll set it off and blow you to smithereens, Alan!"

At recess that afternoon it got worse. My girl friends and I were minding our own business, playing Old Maid with my Braille cards. After we finished, Alan came up and scared me, yelling that I was about to step into a hole. I was embarrassed, until Judy told me it was just another one of his jokes.

That did it! I felt like taking out my glass eyes and throwing them at him! Instead, I shut my eyes tightly and tried to hold back the tears.

As we lined up to leave the playground, I still felt like crying. Why were Alan and his stupid pranks upsetting me so? I nudged Judy. "Do you think I'm . . . handicapped?"

Judy didn't say anything for a while. When the line began to move, she spoke up. "Aimee, I'm not sure what that means. You don't wear hearing aids or crutches. You're not like a poster kid on a telethon, if that's what you mean."

Good old Judy. I was relieved that she didn't think I was handicapped.

After school I headed home, stopping to smell Mrs. Gardner's roses. Scrappy came running to meet me—I could tell it was Scrappy by the jingle of his collar. Just as I was about to turn into our driveway, I heard Grandpa Dudley call from across the street. "Hi, there, Aimee!

Your mom said to tell you she had to run to the store. Do you need any help getting into the house?''

I fumed inside. "No, that's okay."

If I couldn't change Alan's opinion of me, I was certainly going to change Grandpa Dudley's.

I let myself in the house, fixed some chocolate milk, and flicked on the TV. Mom arrived home after a short while, with Grandpa Dudley helping her carry in groceries.

"Aimee, would you mind baby-sitting Matt and Chris tonight? Dad called, and we have to go to a dinner meeting. We'll only be gone a couple hours."

Grandpa Dudley nearly dropped the bag of groceries. "Aimee? Baby-sitting by herself?''

I jerked open the refrigerator door and put the fruit juice and milk away. "I can *do* it, Grandpa. It's only for a couple of hours!''

I'm a *good* baby-sitter. I had helped change Matt and Chris's diapers, fed

50

them, burped them, and put them to bed when they were babies. Now that they're five and six, the boys are used to my being blind. We three are a team.

"Aimee, I've never met a handicapped girl like you. You're amazing!" Grandpa clucked as he walked out the back door.

Thankfully, my mother didn't think I was "amazing." It was an accepted fact in my family that I could be put in charge of Matt and Chris for a couple of hours.

The boys were thrilled to learn I'd be baby-sitting—but it wasn't because they loved me. . . . They loved to *test* me. The games began as soon as Mom and Dad closed the front door behind them.

As I was putting away dinner dishes and getting ready to relax in the living room, I heard the faint click of the back door opening. "Matt, get back in here!"

I heard his little feet come running. "How'd you know, Aimee?" he whined.

I grabbed him and gave him a squeeze. "Because you and your little brother are so noisy. When are you going to learn to be quiet enough to fool me?'' I laughed. ''Remember the time you tried to sneak into my bedroom and change around my clothes so I would get confused?''

Matt giggled and squirmed.

''I caught you, didn't I?'' I said, tickling him. ''Okay, let's see how good you are. Chris?'' I looked toward the couch where I knew he was sitting, building with Legos. ''Are you ready to play our game?''

Chris hopped off the couch and ran toward Matt. The boys giggled and got ready. The air got still and then I could feel one of them put his hand up in front of my face. It was my job to guess how many stubby little fingers he was holding up.

''How many, Aimee?''

''Let's see . . . hmm . . . bring your hand a bit closer, Chris.'' I could feel the air move as his hand drew closer to my face. ''Three! You're holding up three.''

''How did you know?!'' Chris stomped his foot on the ground.

I leaned back on my heels and folded my arms. "I don't know, Chris. I can just, I don't know, feel the air," I said. I grinned at him.

"Do it again!" Matt said. We kept it up for ten minutes. I beat them fifteen out of twenty times.

"Hide-and-seek! Let's play hide-and-seek next!" They were determined to wear me out, but I was just as determined to keep up with them until Dad and Mom got home.

"Okay, now. Remember you can only use this room. One . . . two . . ." I counted up to ten while they scurried to find places to hide.

I have to admit that I loved playing hide-and-seek, too. It was a good test for my radar. And poor Matt and Chris! No matter how hard they tried, I could always hear them breathing behind a chair or catch the sound of their feet and hands rustling on the carpet.

"Where are you?" I called in a sing-song way. "Let's see . . . Where is

Chris?'' I turned around to begin walking to the other side of the living room. Instinctively, I knew that one of those little stinkers was standing right in the middle of the room, not even bothering to hide behind a chair!

"Gotcha!" I reached out and grabbed a giggling little brother. Matt. After we played the game a few more times, we plopped down on the couch to watch TV. Just as we got settled, Chris decided he wanted chicken soup.

"Chicken soup? You just had dinner." I sighed, got up, and led him to the kitchen. "I knew Mom should have made you finish your plate."

I ran my hand over a few of the cans. Fruit cocktail cans were larger than soup cans. I shoved cans of tomato paste out of the way—they were smaller. I put my hand around one can of soup and held it up for Chris to see.

"Tell me the letters," I said. Sometimes I suspected that Chris was more interested in reading the letters than

he was in eating the soup.

"C-H-I. . . ." he said.

He didn't have to go any further. I knew it wasn't chili—the can sloshed like soup. Within minutes I had it opened and the soup heating. I sat next to Chris, watching him eat. Or, I should say, listening to him slurp.

After he finished, I flipped back the plastic crystal on my watch and read the hands. Almost eight-thirty. Time for Mom and Dad to be home soon, and time for Chris and Matt to get ready for bed.

"A story! Please, Aimee, a story!"
Brothers. I sat down on the love seat and
gathered the boys close. They didn't think
of me as handicapped. In fact, they
thought my blindness was a neat thing.
Like Mom and Dad, and even Scrappy,
they loved me, with or without the ability
to see.

I cuddled them and sang and made up
stories until the two of them were fast
asleep in my arms. I should have wakened
them and put them to bed, but I knew our
parents would be home any minute.

Just then I heard a key in the front
door. When I felt Mom and Dad step
through the front door, I raised a finger to
my lips. "Sshhh."

"Everything go okay?" Dad asked as
he lifted Chris off my lap.

I yawned and nodded, happy that, once
again, I had been trusted to do things that
I *knew* I could do.

The next morning I was up early for
school. Gathering my books and patting

Matt and Chris on the head, I stepped out the front door with Scrappy. Halfway down our walk, I heard the scratch of Grandpa Dudley's rake across the street. I felt my watch and realized I had a few extra minutes. Listening for traffic, I walked across the street.

"Good morning, Grandpa," I called as I felt for the curb and slung my duffel bag over my shoulder. "You're getting an early start on your yard work."

"Got to get to it before the sun gets high and hot," he said as I sensed him draw nearer to the fence. "How'd the baby-sitting go?"

"Fine . . . as usual," I answered, trying not to sound sarcastic.

"Well, little girl, you are one amazing lady."

I sighed. In Grandpa's eyes, I was either too crippled to do anything for myself *or* I was Supergirl, the fantastic blind kid, not to be believed unless seen with your very own eyes.

I guess that's the way it will always be.

There will always be a weirdo Alan who could care less. There will always be a Grandpa Dudley who is amazed at whatever I do. And there will always be a Matt and Chris who don't seem to know the difference.

But what do I feel? I wasn't sure of my own feelings about my blindness. Or why else would being called "handicapped" bug me so?

Grandpa interrupted my thoughts. "Did you hear about our new neighbors, the Hollanders?"

"No, I haven't met them."

"You'll really take to the little Hollander girl," he said. I heard him unscrew the cap of his thermos.

"Why is that?"

Grandpa took a long drink and then continued. "Because she's handicapped like you. Well, not exactly like you. Jennifer is her name, and she's in a wheelchair. In fact—" he paused and apparently looked up the street. "Yep, she's sitting on her porch right now."

My face suddenly felt flushed, and I wondered if my cheeks were red. Why did I feel so funny? I should be excited about a new kid on Canwood Street.

I gathered my bag and started walking quickly. "Gotta go, Grandpa . . . I can't be late for school. Bye!"

"Why don't you say hi to Jennifer? I'm sure she'll see you walking by. Her house is the one before Mrs. Gardner's." Grandpa started his rake scratching on the lawn.

A new girl. In a wheelchair. She was . . . *handicapped*. Was she like one of those kids on a telethon? Was she retarded?

When I had walked up nearly half the block, I realized that I must be passing our new neighbor's house. I clenched my duffel bag and kept my head down. Even though I felt certain the new girl could see me from her front porch, I walked on by. When my radar picked up Mrs. Gardner's rosebush, I knew I was out of range. I felt guilty that I hadn't said hello.

All day at school I felt miserable. It didn't help that weirdo Alan was up to his usual antics. During lunchtime, while I was sitting with Judy, he passed behind me and said, "You don't want to sit there . . . not next to the handicapped girl." I couldn't eat any more of my sandwich.

Back in class, I couldn't get Alan and his remark off my mind. *The nerve of him,* I kept thinking. But then it dawned on me. . . .

The problem wasn't Alan. It wasn't even Grandpa Dudley. *You dummy. How could you be so blind?*

All the way home, I kept thinking about Matt and Chris, my mom and dad. Even Scrappy. They accepted me as I was. But did I? *I* knew who *really* had the problem.

I counted my steps to Mrs. Gardner's rosebushes. When my radar told me the bush was next to me, I reached out. Being careful of thorns, I ran my hand over the bush until I found a big bloom. It smelled so sweet. Hoping that Mrs. Gardner wouldn't mind, I snapped the stem. I held the rose tightly and continued on.

When my steps told me I was directly in front of our new neighbor's house, I gathered my courage. "Hello, is anyone home?" I called over the fence.

I heard a girl's voice from the direction of the porch. "Hi, I'm Jennifer. What's your name?"

I breathed a sigh of relief. "Aimee," I said. At that instant I heard Scrappy running up the sidewalk toward me. He bounded up and began whining and licking my arm. "And this is my dog, Scrappy."

"It's nice to meet you. I wish I had a dog."

Suddenly I remembered the rose. "May I give you something?" I asked as I opened the front gate. Slowly I made my way up the unfamiliar walk.

"The steps are right in front of you," Jennifer said. For some reason, it didn't bother me that someone like her— someone who was handicapped—was offering me some help.

I reached for the railing and carefully climbed all four of the front steps. "How did you know I couldn't see?"

"I have other friends who are blind," Jennifer said with a smile in her voice. "I've been in and out of hospitals a lot. I'm in a wheelchair."

I could tell that I was really going to like her.

"I've got red hair and blue eyes," Jennifer went on. "My wheelchair is blue, too."

It was nice of her to offer so much information. Again, I didn't seem to mind that she wanted to help.

"Oh, I almost forgot. This is for you." I held out the rose. She took the stem and I heard her sniff.

"Thank you," she said softly. After a pause she continued. "I saw you go by this morning. I'm glad you decided to stop. Sometimes it's, well—it's lonely."

"You mean being the new kid on the block?" I offered.

"Sometimes it's just lonely being . . . being handicapped. You must know what I mean?"

I knew exactly what she meant. For the first time, I thought I might have found someone who could understand exactly how I felt.

I nodded my head. "Yes, I know what you mean about being handicapped. I guess we've got a lot in common."

Handicapped. I had used the word to describe not only Jennifer, but myself. And I actually told someone in a wheelchair that I had things in common with her!

"I've got to go or my mom will wonder where I am. See you later," I said. Scrappy and I made our way back to the front walk.

"Bye," Jennifer called. "Thanks for the rose. And thanks for stopping."

"See you later." I waved good-bye.

I tousled Scrappy's hair and briskly walked toward home. The oak trees smelled wet and sweet. The roses were fragrant. The sky, I imagined, must be blue. I waved hello to Grandpa Dudley. Yes, Canwood Street was a wonderful place to live. I thought that everything was perfect before—Mrs. Gardner's roses, Mr. Espey's tomatoes, the oak trees, our friends. But now it was even more special. After all, not every street has two special, handicapped kids like Jennifer and me.

A VOICE FOR JAMIE

A church camp. How did *I* ever end up on a bus going to church camp? It would have been neater to go to a deaf camp with friends I could understand . . . friends who use sign language. But that's what I get for hanging around Kristen. She has a way of making me do things I think are icky.

And as we bounced along in an old church bus, the whole idea of spending a week with a bunch of her hearing girl friends at camp was bo-or-ring. I thought hearing girls were stuck up. They always think they're so much better, just because they can hear.

Oh, I guess I'd better introduce myself. My name is Jamie. I have a mop of brown curly hair, I like to read Laura Ingalls Wilder books, I love M & Ms, and I'm deaf. My friend Kristen, who could pass for my twin (except she likes Snickers bars), is deaf, too. We got to know each other at school. That's where Kristen cornered me and asked me to come to this church camp.

Anyway, Kristen and I are friends, maybe even best friends. We can both read lips, although I wish I were as good at lipreading as Kristen. And we're both super at sign language. At school we have races to see who can finger spell through the alphabet the fastest! The only thing I *don't* like about Kristen is, well . . . she's always talking about God. And she's always nice—even to hearing girls.

"Hey, Jamie." Kristen turned to me and spoke in sign language. *"You're going to love camp. And you'll really love Camille, our sign language interpreter. She's an awesome counselor. She even*

uses slang in her sign language . . . not like our English teachers at school!''

Suddenly we realized that someone was standing next to our seat. I looked up into the face of a girl with freckles and a French braid. She had been sitting across the aisle, watching Kristen and me sign to one another. Nervously, she shoved a message scrawled in pencil into Kristen's hands.

Can you guys teach me some signs?

''Sure, we'll teach you some signs,'' Kristen spoke up. The girl with freckles seemed surprised that Kristen could speak. ''And yes, we can read your lips . . . if you don't talk too fast or hide your mouth.'' Boy, Kristen sure has more guts than I do. I'm always afraid to use my voice, since I can't hear myself speak. And lots of times when I've tried to speak, I've gotten laughed at. I must sound funny.

67

"Wow, neat! What are you going to teach me?" the freckled girl asked, excitedly biting her nails. Actually, I didn't catch the first part of her sentence—I couldn't see her lips through her fingers. She had already flunked Kristen's first lesson! What an airhead.

Kristen, smiling and outgoing as ever, showed the girl how to finger spell her name. I watched Kristen's fingers slowly spell out M-A-R-C-I-E. Marcie was Freckle Face's name.

68

Marcie seemed thrilled with her new talent. She turned to the rest of her hearing friends at the front of the bus and proudly finger spelled.

Big deal, so she can finger spell her name, I thought. *Now Marcie will think she knows everything.*

She whipped back around and blurted another question. "Why do you two wear hearing aids if you can't hear me speak?"

What is this, deaf awareness week? I casually smoothed my hair over my ears. I thought I had done a good job of hiding my hearing aids when I combed my hair.

Kristen answered Marcie as if she had given this information a hundred times before. "Hearing aids," she said with a smile, "help us know when something's making a lot of noise . . . like this bus."

Or like you, Marcie, I thought.

Marcie half-stared at Kristen, letting the answer sink in. But she wasn't done. "What's it like being deaf?" she piped up. I glanced at her friends. They were flipping through comic books, but I could tell they were straining to hear.

Out of nowhere, I snapped, "WELL, WHAT'S IT LIKE BEING HEARING?"

Marcie took a step back as her friends shrank in their seats. "Wh-what was that?" Marcie asked, as if she didn't catch my words.

Oh, rats! *She didn't understand me.* I can't believe I even let sound come out of my mouth! Like I said, I hardly talk at all, especially around hearing girls. I probably sounded like a real nerd.

Kristen jumped in with a smile and an answer. "Marcie, you probably can't explain what it's like to hear . . . and we can't explain what it's like *not* to hear." Marcie and her friends seemed to relax a little.

Kristen, in her cheery way, kept talking. "Even though we can't hear, we enjoy lots of the same things you do. We can watch TV—"

Marcie flopped in her seat, leaned on her elbow, and said, "Wait a minute. If you can't hear, how can you enjoy, like,

'The Cosby Show'?'' We had to strain to read Marcie's lips because the bus was bouncing so much.

"Easy. Jamie and I have a decoder—a little box on top of the TV that sort of translates words into writing on the TV screen. Right, Jamie?'' Kristen spoke and signed at the same time so I would be sure to understand. I just nodded, as if I could have cared less about TVs or decoders. It seemed to me that Marcie was being awfully nosy.

That didn't bother Kristen. With her same smile, she charged right ahead, "And we love to play charades and act out stories.'' Then Kristen got a bright idea. *"Hey, Jamie.''* She turned to me and signed as she spoke. *"Do your impression of Bill Cosby dancing!''*

I shrugged my shoulders and gave her a dirty look, even though I didn't mean it. "Come on, Jamie,'' Kristen said out loud. "Please. Do that neat dance!''

Marcie jumped up. "Can you really dance like Bill Cosby? Let's see!'' She was jabbering so fast I couldn't catch every word, but I got the idea.

"Yeah, Jamie, we love that crazy dance he does. Please!" Marcie's friends were kneeling on their seats, pleading.

Up until then, I had been pretty quiet around these dumb hearing girls. Here was my chance to show them I was as good as they were—if not better. Anyway, I *did* enjoy acting and imitating others. My deaf friends say I'm really good at impressions. I looked around, took a deep breath, and rose to my feet.

I don't know where I got the nerve, but I began my routine—twisting and jerking like Bill Cosby right there in the aisle of the bus. When I whirled around, I saw Marcie's friends sliding off their seats, laughing hysterically. I knew it! They weren't laughing with me. They were laughing *at* me! I threw myself back into my seat.

The bus jostled down the road as the laughter settled. Marcie still looked as though she was about to burst with

72

questions. Finally she spoke up again.

"Kristen, are you ever sorry you can't hear?"

That time I caught every word on Marcie's lips. I quickly focused on Kristen. This was one answer I wanted to hear!

Kristen squinted, thinking, and then spoke. "Sometimes it's hard being deaf . . . but I'm not really . . . sorry. Besides, I feel closer to God." There was a long pause. I looked around at the girls in the bus and could tell that it was quiet.

The bus rounded a corner and turned onto a dirt road which bordered the edge of a woods. As we crested the hill we could see the camp, complete with bunkhouses, a meeting hall, a dining room, and a corral. Our bus pulled into a gravel parking lot and jerked to a stop. Before the driver could stand up and shout instructions, kids were climbing over each other to grab their sleeping bags, pillows, and jackets. Kristen and I reached for our things under the seat and piled out.

Immediately I saw a short, pretty blonde girl wave at Kristen. I figured she must be Camille, our interpreter. Hmmm. I wondered if she was as good at signing as Kristen claimed.

"Hi, Kristen," Camille signed and gave her a big hug. *"This must be your friend Jamie from school. Hi, Jamie!"* she signed at me.

"Yeah, hi," I sloppily signed back.

"Isn't it terrific being at camp?" Her fingers flew.

"We'll see," I signed, and then added, *"You can talk, you know. I can read lips. Not as well as Kristen does, but I'll manage."*

"Great! That's good to know!" Camille spoke up while signing at the same time. "Okay, girls, keep close to me so you can read my lips. I've got to organize this bunch of monkeys."

She laughed, looking at the rest of the kids who were slapping name tags on each other and passing around registration forms and pencils.

74

"Girls! Girls!" Camille yelled. "We have cabin assignments here!" In a few minutes Camille had the entire bus divided into neat groups. "And Marcie, you, Tracie, and Kelly are with Kristen and Jamie in my cabin. Got it?"

"Neat-o!" Marcie jumped up and down, clapping. "We're with you two," she shouted at Kristen and me.

Hearing kids . . . just who I wanted to room with.

I stuffed my sleeping bag under my arm and followed Kristen to our cabin. I was nearly pushed through the door by Tracie and Kelly, who raced to claim the best bunks. Tracie scrambled for one by the window. Kelly claimed the top bunk in the corner. Marcie quickly sat down on the bed nearest the bathroom. I tossed my sleeping bag on the bunk that was left. I could tell this was going to be a rowdy cabin.

I pulled some jeans and sweat shirts out of my duffel bag and folded them in one of the dresser drawers. Kristen was talking in sign language with Camille, their fingers flying a mile a minute. Why was Kristen always so disgustingly happy? And how could she trust Camille so much—someone who could *hear?*

As Camille helped the others unpack, I cornered Kristen. I didn't want anybody to eavesdrop, so I spoke only in sign language.

"Something's been bothering me ever since the bus ride."

Kristen seemed surprised. *"What's the matter?"*

"What's the big deal about God? You're deaf, Kristen. You're supposed to be mad at Him." I glanced over my shoulder to make sure Camille was nowhere in sight.

"I don't know how to explain it, Jamie," Kristen answered. *"You're deaf, too. You know what it's like. . . . It's quieter. So much other stuff is blocked out—my little brother's whining . . . people complaining . . . even my parents arguing. So I can 'hear' God better."*

She pointed to her ears. *"Do you know what I mean?"*

I looked at my friend sadly. No, I didn't know what she meant.

"Let's go check out the camp on our way to dinner," Camille announced while signing to Kristen and me.

The girls kicked their suitcases under the bunks, grabbed their sweat shirts, and bolted out the door.

I knotted my sweat shirt sleeves around my waist and followed. We headed for the swimming pool and stuck our toes in the water. From there we took a path to the stables and fed carrots to the horses. We passed by the meeting hall and pressed our noses against the windows to get a good look. Once again, Marcie was babbling off a lot of questions.

"What a motor mouth that girl is," I signed to Kristen as we stood directly in front of Marcie. Miss Freckle Face could have no idea what I was saying about her in our secret language.

Kristen quickly grabbed my fingers

with one hand and signed to me with the other. *"Hey . . . let's not gossip. Marcie's really trying."*

I felt a little ashamed. I knew it was wrong to say nasty things in sign language in front of somebody.

From the meeting hall, we headed toward the dining room. Our group played follow-the-leader—a dumb game Kristen obviously enjoyed playing with her hearing friends. I tagged behind.

The dining room was a big log cabin with elk horns and deer heads hung on the walls. Kids were everywhere. I stuck close to Kristen.

During dinner, Marcie had more questions. "Are my lips easy to read, Kristen?"

"Well, let's see . . ." Kristen examined Marcie's lips. "Yeah, your upper lip isn't too short . . . and you don't mumble. I'd say you're easy to lip read."

Except when your mouth is full of spaghetti, I thought as I watched her chew. I wasn't kidding.

Everybody was chewing, so I just kept to myself. Although Camille often put down her knife and fork to sign, she got distracted with Tracie and Kelly, who were throwing peas at each other. The only one I felt comfortable with was Kristen.

That night we were in the bathroom getting ready for bed. Kristen and I were about to brush our teeth when I noticed Tracie and Kelly looking at us. In fact, Tracie started to say something to Kristen and me and then halfway through her sentence, she put her hand over her mouth. She didn't *want* us to read her lips! I quickly looked the other way and started squeezing toothpaste on my brush.

Just then Kelly started mouthing something else at us, but we had no idea what she was saying—her mouth was stuffed full of toothpaste. They were doing it just to be mean.

"Cut it out, you guys!" Marcie angrily punched Tracie on the shoulder. She turned to Kelly and threatened, "I'm going to tell Camille on you!"

I kept brushing my teeth, pretending nothing had happened. But inside I was fighting back tears. Then I shot a look at Kristen, and I couldn't believe my eyes.

Kristen was laughing. She was laughing at Tracie and Kelly. Then she started flinging toothpaste at them! That gave Tracie and Kelly more giggles. Kristen signed at them, *"You two have toothpaste for brains!"* Of course, they had no idea what she was saying. The two of them stood there looking confused and a little angry.

Kristen shook her finger at them and then spoke up, "I just wanted to give you an idea of how it feels to be left out. Teasing can hurt." But she smiled as she spoke.

I was amazed. Kristen had handled the whole thing like a pro.

Camille entered the bathroom. "Okay, what's going on, you guys?"

"Oh, nothing. Just a little fun,"

Kristen answered. Tracie and Kelly had sheepish looks on their faces.

"Okay, then. Let's get it together for cabin time," Camille said, clapping. She turned to me, and I tried to hide my hurt feelings. *"Anything wrong?"* she signed, putting her arm around me and giving me a squeeze. I shook my head no.

During cabin time, some of the girls sat on the edge of their bunks, while others sat cross-legged on the floor. I lay on my side in bed, my eyes mostly on Camille. She joked with everyone, even Kristen and me. We played games, and she asked a lot of questions like what was going on at school, who had the worst little brother, and what happened last week on Saturday morning cartoons. I could see why Kristen loved Camille, and why she trusted her. And she was right—Camille definitely didn't sign like our English teachers at school!

Marcie showed how she could finger spell not only her name, but everybody's name in the whole cabin. I thought back on the bathroom scene. It struck me that at least Marcie was making an effort. And I realized something else—I had made no effort at all.

Cabin time began to quiet down. Camille, sitting cross-legged on her bed, opened her Bible. I settled in for something superboring.

"Prayer is so neat," Camille signed and spoke. "It's our way of talking to God. And isn't it great that He actually listens? And that He understands sign language, too?" She winked at Kristen and me.

Hmm, I never thought of that before.

"But conversation is two-way. We have to hear Him, too. How do we do that?" Camille asked.

Marcie raised her hand. "By reading the Bible."

"That's right. But more than just reading, we have to really *listen*. That's the only way to have good communication. Look here." Camille pointed to the Bible on her lap. " 'I am the Good Shepherd. I know My sheep and My sheep know Me. . . . They will *listen* to My voice.' "

Marcie was scratching her head, thinking. Kelly was staring at the ceiling. Tracie was examining her toes. Kristen had a faraway look on her face, as though she understood exactly what Camille was reading.

Do they hear His voice? What does it sound like? I strained to hear what Kristen seemed to hear. Then I rolled over on my bunk and sighed. *There's no voice talking to me.*

A couple days later Camille took us on a nature walk. I couldn't stop thinking about hearing God's voice. We passed by a grove of pines. The wind was moving the branches, but I couldn't hear the pines whispering as I had read they did in one of Laura Ingalls Wilder's books. We spied a woodpecker attacking an oak tree. I saw his beak drilling like a jackhammer, but I could only imagine the sound. Camille led us beside a big waterfall and covered her ears as though the water was making a loud roar. But I wasn't certain what "roar" meant, either. After all, lions roar. Does a waterfall sound like a lion?

Later on we put on our swimsuits and headed for the pool. The hearing girls played Marco Polo, but I sat on a lounge chair and watched. I couldn't hear anyone shout "Marco!", so how could I play?

Kristen came and sat next to me. *"It's hard not being able to play, isn't it?"* she signed.

I leaned on my wrists and nodded. A long stretch of silence hung between us.

Kristen suddenly sat up. *"Jamie, I forgot to tell you. Tonight is team competition night, and I heard we're going to play charades. Let's you and I surprise everybody!"*

Charades! I didn't want to admit it, but instantly I was on pins and needles. Kristen was right—we would wow 'em!

After supper the log and timber meeting hall was jam-packed with groups from

84

every cabin. Teams were competing in every corner of the room. I couldn't hear what was going on, but it seemed like there was a lot of noise in the hall. Our corner was ready to go.

We knelt in a huddle across from the opposing team. Everybody was scribbling ideas on paper, poking one another and whispering. I could tell that the other cabins must be coming up with some good ideas for charades. Several times the girls rolled over, giggling and clapping.

Camille stood between our two teams and blew a whistle. First up was Marcie. She walked over to the other group to take her slip of paper. She unfolded it, read the message, and stuffed the paper in her pocket, rolling her eyes.

"Come on, Marcie," Tracie called. Kristen and I grinned at each other. We were ready to guess.

Camille clicked her stopwatch, and Marcie nervously began to act out her charade. She stretched and swayed, her arms floating like . . . *branches of a tree*

. . . *a* . . . *willow tree!* Just to make certain, I quickly signed to Kristen what I thought was the answer. Her face lit up and she nodded quickly.

I jumped to my feet and whipped out the answer in sign language. *"Wind in the Willows!"*

"Jamie's answer is *The Wind in the Willows!"* Camille shouted the interpretation.

Marcie jumped up and down like a kangaroo. I was right! Everybody on my team patted my shoulders. Camille announced our time—twenty seconds.

A girl with curly black hair rose from the opposing team, walked over to us, and took a slip of paper. She studied her message as she went back to her team. When the whistle blew and the stopwatch started, she began playacting her charade. Twenty . . . thirty . . . almost sixty seconds passed before her team finally guessed correctly—*Charlie and the Chocolate Factory.*

Once again, our team was on. It was Kelly's turn. She skipped in a circle and whistled, leaning over and patting us all on our heads. *She looks like . . . "Snow White and the Seven Dwarfs."* Again I was quick to my feet. " 'Snow White and the Seven Dwarfs,' " I spoke out loud before my hands even started to sign. *Good grief, I spoke out loud!*

Several girls on the other team collapsed against each other, whining and moaning.

"Hurray for Jamie!" Marcie, Kristen,

Kelly, and Tracie danced around me.

"Boy, Jamie, you are absolutely amazing!" Kelly said, as she shook my shoulders. Kristen had to interpret that sentence for me—Kelly was shaking me so hard, her lips looked like jiggling Jell-O!

Our teams went back and forth, acting out the charades and guessing as quickly as we could. After the third round, it was my turn. I unfolded my slip of paper and read my charade. I knew exactly how it should be acted out.

I walked up to my team, took a deep breath, and waited for Camille to give the signal. Then I acted as though I were primping in front of a mirror, putting on lipstick and admiring myself like Miss America. The next minute I was hunched and snarling, acting like a werewolf.

" 'Beauty and the Beast'!" Kristen jumped up and shouted. Hurray! I knew Kristen would do it. If anybody could understand my body language, it was definitely my deaf friend!

An hour passed quickly. It was no contest—our cabin won the entire team competition night! We grabbed each other and bounced up and down, dancing in a circle. I couldn't hear the applause, but I could feel it. I saw everyone's mouth moving, and I knew they were shouting and laughing.

I also knew they weren't laughing at me.

The girls began stomping and chanting, "We're number one. We're number one!" I felt the vibrations all through me, and I stomped right in time with them. "We're number one!" Kristen was yelling. I found myself shouting, too, "We're number one!" I couldn't believe I was having so much fun using my voice! I wasn't embarrassed. I didn't care what I sounded like. For the first time since I got off the camp bus, I was glad that Kristen had talked me into coming.

I looked up and noticed Camille. Our eyes met for a moment, and I thought I saw tears in her eyes. For a split second, it didn't matter that I couldn't hear and others could.

After the winners were announced and refreshments were served, all the kids left the meeting hall and walked over to the campfire. Kristen and I strolled together. Suddenly, Marcie came from behind and flung her arms around each of us. We found an empty log and sat, huddling together with the rest of the girls from our cabin.

The kids quieted down, the camp speaker stood up, and Camille positioned herself to interpret the message. Kristen pulled her flashlight out of her jacket and focused it on Camille. Neither of us wanted to miss a single word. For the first time I actually wanted to hear what someone had to say about the Bible. I glanced around the campfire. Everybody else seemed warm and happy to be there, too.

Camille's hands moved like a windmill as she signed the speaker's words.
" *'What do you think? If a man has a*

hundred sheep and one wanders away
from the rest, won't he leave the ninety-
nine on the hillside and set out to look for
the one who has wandered away? Yes,
and if he should chance to find it, I assure
you he is more delighted over that one
than he is over the ninety-nine who never
wandered away.' "

I looked over at Kristen, who smiled at
me.

" 'You can understand, then, that it is
never the will of your Father in heaven
that a single one of these little ones
should be lost.' " The speaker paused and
closed her Bible. Camille rested her
hands, waiting for her to continue. *"Have
you ever felt lost before? Well, if you
have, listen for God's voice. He not only
cares about the whole flock, but He cares
for you."*

I felt even warmer inside, and I knew it
wasn't because of the fire. The speaker
began to pray. The kids around us bowed
their heads and closed their eyes. Kristen
and I fixed our eyes on Camille's hands to

hear what the speaker was praying.

After the fire died down into glowing embers, we all stretched, yawned, and began to wander back to our cabins. I watched Kristen massage Camille's arm muscles. Our poor interpreter was zonked from so much signing.

Camille smiled at me, and the truth hit—even though there were far many more hearing kids at camp, Camille cared for *me*. Just as if I were that single lost sheep.

Tracie and Kelly were walking ahead of me. One of them jabbed the other in the ribs, whispered, and then stopped to turn around.

"We're, uh . . . sorry about what happened in the bathroom, Jamie." Tracie exaggerated her words too much.

I shrugged my shoulders and nodded. Before, I would have gloated over such an apology. Now I realized it was no big deal. The toothpaste incident seemed like ages ago. Like Kristen, I was beginning to feel . . . quieter inside. More peaceful.

I stopped along the dirt path and listened to the quiet. The trees moved, and the wind touched my face. I stopped imagining what whispering pines must sound like. Instead, I began to enjoy the quiet. Not just around me, but *inside* of me. Perhaps, after all, God's voice was talking to me, too.

Back at the cabin, most of the girls were already in their bunks. It was dark, so I couldn't tell if anyone was talking, but it didn't matter. I had a lot to think about. Camille hugged me and Kristen, and we crawled into our bunks.

After lights out, when I was sure that almost everyone was asleep, I shined my flashlight on the ceiling, a signal to Kristen that I wanted to tell her something. When I saw her flashlight twinkle back, I stuffed mine between my knees and moved my hands in the beam of light.

"For the first time, I can hear God."

Wasn't it fun getting to know my friends? Were you surprised (and maybe a little embarrassed) when Josh fell out of his wheelchair? How do you think Jamie felt when the girls at camp made fun of her? And wasn't it neat that Aimee could tell which socks she had on by feeling them? (Try standing in front of your closet, closing your eyes, and touching the sleeves and collars of your shirts. Can you guess which ones are which?)

I learned that Kristen, Josh, and the rest were just everyday sorts of people, very much like you. They have the same fearful feelings, the same sense of right and wrong, the same love for games and surprises, and the very same ability to reach out to God and others.

Do you remember the apostle Paul in the Bible? He had a disability, although we don't know what it was. And guess what he said? ''I can do all things through Christ who gives me strength'' (Philippians 4:13). It doesn't matter whether we're in a wheelchair or can do *the best cartwheel in school—we all have times when we feel afraid, have doubts, or do something stupid. But like the kids in these stories, I know you, too, can do many more things than you ever dreamed possible.*

Wouldn't you like to be friends with someone like Josh or Aimee? You can! You may know someone in your own neighborhood—someone who is disabled—who would like to be your friend. I just know you won't be as shy about meeting that person, now that you've met my friends in this book.

Try it—give someone your smile and warm hello. If you're afraid, just ask God to help you. It may be the start of an exciting new adventure!

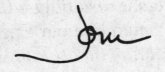